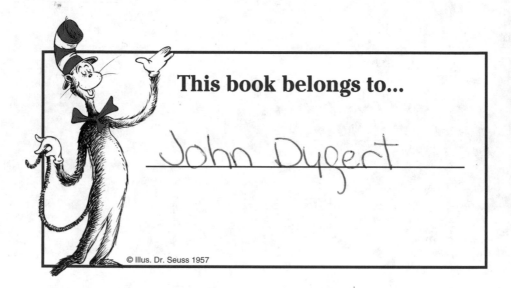

This book belongs to...

John Dygert

© Illus. Dr. Seuss 1957

GROLIER
B O O K S

For Will and Franny

—M.C.

6 Sticks

By Molly Coxe

Library of Congress Cataloging-in-Publication Data
Coxe, Molly. Six sticks / by Molly Coxe. p.   cm.   (Early step into reading + math)
SUMMARY: Depicts various things that can be made with six sticks, from a tall mouse to a trapeze for fleas.
ISBN 0-679-88689-3 (pbk.) — ISBN 0-679-98689-8 (lib. bdg.) 1. Geometry—Juvenile literature.   2. Six (The number)—Juvenile literature.   [1. Shape.] I. Title. II. Series. QA445.5.C646 1999 516.2—dc21 97-7972

Printed in the United States of America   10 9 8 7 6 5 4 3 2 1

A Bright & Early Book
From BEGINNER BOOKS
A Division of Random House, Inc.

Random House 🏠 New York

6 sticks.

6 sticks.

6 sticks make 6 flags.

6 sticks make 6 whiskers.

6 sticks make…

2 swings.

6 sticks make 3 T's.

6 sticks make

2 snowflakes.

6 sticks make

3 pairs of skis.

6 sticks make
4 legs,
1 body,
and 1 sword!

6 sticks make

2 tents.

1 for a mad mouse.

1 for a sad mouse.

6 sticks...

make…

1 mouse
clubhouse!